Sinclair

Acquisition Series Prologue

Celia Aaron

Sinclair

Acquisition Series Prologue

Celia Aaron

Cover art by L.J. at mayhemcovercreations.com

Editing by J. Brooks

ISBN: 1533259798
ISBN-13: 978-1533259790

Other Books By Celia Aaron

Counsellor
The Acquisition Series, Book 1

Magnate
The Acquisition Series, Book 2

Sovereign
The Acquisition Series, Book 3

***

Cash Remington and the Missing Heiress
Sexy Dreadfuls, Book 1

***

Cleat Chaser
Co-written with Sloane Howell

***

The Forced Series

***

The Hard and Dirty Holidays

***

Zeus
Taken by Olympus, Book 1

CHAPTER ONE

BLOOD STREAKED MY MOTHER'S face and dripped down the front of her yellow sun dress. Screams ricocheted through the night, and flames leapt into the sky from the neighboring property.

The house was eerily quiet. Mom and I were the only ones inside. I blinked hard, trying to erase the horrors I'd seen from my vision. But when I opened my eyes, Mom was still there, still staring down at me.

"Why are you crying?" She grabbed my wrist and yanked me toward the wide front doors.

I wiped my tears with my free hand as she lifted the bar from the doors and tossed it onto the floor, marring the wooden planks. She wrenched the door inward. The screams were no longer muffled. Agonized cries rose from the fields of sugar cane that stretched as far as I could see in the pale moonlight. The neighboring fields were on fire, the acrid smoke making my eyes water even more.

She ripped me down the front steps. I yelled as my ankle turned on the last stair, but she only pulled me harder toward the fields.

"Mom, please!" I tried to dig my heels into the hardened dirt.

She whirled and stabbed her index finger into my chest. "Don't you *ever* beg *anyone*! You hear me? You're a Vinemont. You don't cry. You don't beg. You do what you have to do to keep this family on top. Do you understand me?"

My chest ached where she'd poked me, and her harsh words only made me cry harder. "I-I'm sorry, Mom. Let's go back."

The blood around her mouth had crusted a deep brown, but the streaks along her cheeks glimmered like fresh paint. She bent down and wiped a tear from my face with her thumb.

"There is no going back." She stared into my eyes, a cruel smirk on her face. My mother, but I didn't recognize her. Something had happened to her during the last year. Something bad. "No going back. Never. Never again."

"Mom." I took her hand. "Let's just go. Let's go. Please!"

Her stinging slap rocked me back on my heels. "Not yet."

I clutched my cheek. She'd never hit me before. I couldn't hold back the sob that shot from my lungs. I wanted to wake up. It had to be a nightmare.

She dashed to the edge of the sugar cane field and yanked down a stalk. She pulled off a set of green leaves and turned back to me as her foreman sauntered around the side of the house. Two men behind him dragged a third.

"Señora Vinemont!"

She grinned and took my hand, pulling me back toward the house. The man lifted his head, a bloody gash running along his bald pate.

"Rebecca?" He blinked, his eyes teary from the heavy smoke, or perhaps from something else.

"That's Sovereign, to you." Her voice was hard, like stone grinding against stone, but she curtsied like a little girl. "Edward Rose. So nice to see you again." To the foreman, she said, "Take him inside."

The men dragged Mr. Rose up the front steps as we followed behind, my hand clamped firmly in my mother's strong grip. A cold tingle ran down my spine. Instead of going inside, I wanted to escape. But the screams in the fields at my back kept me hemmed in. There was nowhere to run. And my mother was gone, though she looked the same, had the same voice.

Once we were all inside, the foreman barred the heavy front doors again. The men set Mr. Rose on his feet. Mother circled around him, her skirt swaying as she perused him with eyes that were foreign to me. Gone was the mother who used to read to me, hold me in her lap, and chase me around the house when I rode my bike indoors. This woman—the one with the cold blue eyes and the blood-streaked face—was a stranger.

She circled Mr. Rose one more time as he finally stood on his own. His eyes remained downcast.

"Sovereign, I-I—"

"Shh." She stood in front of him as the other men smirked and backed away. Mr. Rose swayed, but stayed on his feet. Then she held out her right hand, her fair skin still delicate even though it was tinged with crimson.

The foreman put a pistol in her hand, and she handed the sugar cane leaves to me.

Mr. Rose began to quake and shake his head, the gash oozing blood down to his ear. "I-I'm sorry about the supply issues. I promise, it won't happen again. Now that you're Sovereign, I w-won't … please"—his voice broke—"please, Sovereign, I beg you, please."

Mother pulled me forward so I stood next to her. She handled the gun with delicate, deadly fingers.

"I think you know it's too late for that." She pulled the hammer back, the click somehow loud even with the noise outside.

"It doesn't have to be." Mr. Rose finally looked up, his mouth turned down at the corners, his chin quivering. "I'll give you whatever you want."

"I'm already *taking* what I want." She pressed the gun against his forehead.

He pulled away, but the two men were on him, holding him in place by his elbows.

I grabbed her hand. "Mom?"

"This is what you need to learn, Sinclair. This is what you have to be." She never took her eyes from Mr. Rose.

"No." Mr. Rose cried and sniffed, a line of snot rolling to his lips. "Please. My family."

Mother laughed. "Dead. All dead. All gone. Did you have fun at the Christmas trial?"

He shook his head. "Wh-what?"

"Answer my question. Did you have fun at the Christmas trial?"

"I only did what everyone else—"

She cracked the butt of the gun along his cheek. "I asked you if *you* had fun. Not everyone else."

"I-I- don't remember... Please, Rebecca."

She cracked him again in the same spot and he screamed, but the men held him steady as more blood mixed with his tears.

"Yes, Sovereign. I did. Yes."

"Remember my Acquisition? Remember what you did to her? I can still hear her screams as you violated her, hurt her. I know every word you said, every time you told her to take it and called her a slut, every time you said she was a cunt who loved getting fucked in her ass. Do you remember all that?"

My stomach lurched, and I turned to the side. What little contents I had in my stomach emptied onto the floor in one powerful heave. The foreman laughed and stepped back.

"Sinclair!" Mom grabbed my chin and wrenched my face around to hers. "Watch every moment of this. Don't turn away. You have to learn."

I shuddered at her touch, her nails digging into my

face. "Okay."

"Better. Now, where was I?" She tapped the gun barrel on her cheek. "Oh, right. You raping my Acquisition over, and over, and over again."

Mr. Rose didn't respond, but his eyes pleaded with Mom. I clutched the sugar cane leaves until my fingers broke through them.

Mom backed up a few feet and pulled me with her. "Don't look away, Sinclair," she said as she raised the gun. "Never look away."

"Please—" Mr. Rose's plea was cut off by the deafening roar of the pistol. His right cheek exploded, the white of his teeth showing through, and he slumped to the ground. The men who'd been holding him backed away and wiped his blood from their faces.

I screamed. The sound ripped from me as Mom gave the gun back to the foreman with a steady hand.

The foreman nodded and smiled. "*Muy bien*, Señora Vinemont."

The cry died in my throat as my lungs burned for want of air. I gasped and stared at Mr. Rose, unmoving on the floor. One of the men kicked him over onto his back. Only one eye remained intact, and it stared at me. If his mouth could move, it would tell me this was all my fault somehow.

"Get him out of here and clean this up." She waved a dismissive hand at the men and grabbed my upper arm.

"Mom?" I let her pull me to the dining room. She shoved me into a chair, took the one across from me, then snatched the sugar cane leaves from my numb fingers. My ears rang in a high note, nothing like the deep sound of the gun. And I couldn't stop the tears.

"Mommy?" I needed her more than I'd ever needed anything. Where was she?

The woman across from me smiled. "Hold your hand out."

I shook so hard my teeth chattered. "N-no."

"Sinclair, put your hand on the table." Her voice darkened. "Now."

I swallowed hard and placed my hand on the edge of the table. She reached across and yanked it so I was leaning over, my arm outstretched. My tears plopped onto the dark wood beneath me.

She plucked a sugar cane leaf and felt along the stiff side. As she slid her finger down the sharp edge, red welled up from a smooth cut on her fingertip.

She smiled and placed her other hand, palm down, next to mine. "Now, let's begin."

CHAPTER TWO

"HAVE YOU HEARD WHO'S gotten picked for this year?" Judge Montagnet sipped his bourbon, his black robe open as he lounged in his chambers.

I pulled on my sleeves, ensuring that my cuff links were perfectly turned.

"No, Judge, I sure haven't. Should be an interesting year with Cal in charge." I smiled. It was mechanical. Sometimes I would have to actively think about how a normal person would react to a statement or an action, and then attempt to mold my response in the same fashion.

"I really can't wait. Christmas trial is always my favorite. Did you attend during the year Cal won?" He shifted his hips higher, the law clerk between his legs making sloppy noises as he bobbed his head on the judge's cock.

"No, I'm afraid to say the sugar business called me away to foreign lands quite a bit that year." I finished my bourbon and set the glass on the polished wood table to my right.

Judge Montagnet closed his eyes and gripped the young man's head, pulling him close. After a series of choking noises and some low grunts from the judge, it was over.

The law clerk sat back, sputtering and gasping for air. He wiped his sleeve across his eyes, and it came away wet with tears.

No pity for him welled in my deadened heart. I had no concept of what that word even meant. Was it a feeling? A thought? I was better off without it, not that I had a choice in the matter. I couldn't miss something I'd never experienced in the first place.

Boredom swirled around me, and I wanted to get the hearing over with as soon as possible. As the district attorney for the parish, I had to prosecute all criminal offenses while Judge Montagnet made a show of presiding over the trials. The job only became fun when I found a really nasty rat and made him squeal.

Luckily, I'd found just such a rat in Leon Rousseau. His arraignment was set on the docket, and I had big plans to investigate every scrap of paper and every dime flowing to and from his accounts. Making his life a living hell would amuse me for a time, at least until I found something better.

Judge Montagnet zipped up and patted the law clerk on the head. "Good work. Run along now and let them know I'll be on the bench in a moment."

The clerk stood, crimson painting his cheeks, and left.

"I guess that's my cue." I rose as the judge straightened his robes and smoothed his white hair.

"I'll see you out there. Anyone you want me to roast today?"

I smirked. "I think I can handle the roasting at the moment. You've had all the fun so far. Now it's my turn."

He smiled, his wrinkles turning his thin skin into accordions around his mouth. "I sure have."

I fastened my top coat button and strode out into the courtroom. The bailiff nodded at me as I skirted the bench and headed toward the counsel tables. The public defender had already set up his files on his side. My side was bare. I knew my cases; no files necessary.

I scanned the gallery behind the short wooden wall separating the front and back of the courtroom. Leon Rousseau sat and stared at me with his beady eyes. But he wasn't what caught my attention. I didn't break my step, but I couldn't take my eyes off the redhead sitting beside him.

Her head was bowed, and she wore a black suit, the skirt too long for my tastes and the cut too modest. So prim and proper. I wanted to toy with her, bat her around like a cat playing with a mortally wounded mouse.

I'd never been drawn to another human being. The sensation was odd, irritating. Even so, her red hair would look perfect clenched in my fist, and I had to take a sharp breath at the thought of her skin bearing marks from my belt.

I walked the remaining steps to my table, but she didn't look up. The flame of desire began to burn lower when I realized she was too tame. I would break her in an instant, and I didn't want to play with broken toys. Pity.

She looked up at me. Her green eyes pinned me to the spot, and my heart kicked against my ribs. She was more. So much more. Her hateful gaze scorched me like a firebrand, and I wanted the burn. I wanted to give it back to her, make her scream and call my name—in agony or pleasure, or that perfect mix of both. She held me there, as if the hate in her eyes had snared me in a trap.

"Counsellor Vinemont?" Judge Montagnet's voice echoed around the wood-paneled walls. "Which case would you like to handle first?"

I cut my eyes from her to Leon Rousseau and back again. He gripped her hand with his. A name flitted around my mind. A daughter, he had a daughter. *Stella.* I smirked as her name came to me, and she kicked her chin up a notch in response.

Still meeting her gaze, I called, "Judge, I'd like to take Leon Rousseau's case first, if that's all right with you."

When her eyes fell, the beast who lived in my hollow

heart roared. She was fire, but she could be contained. Dominated. By me. And I already felt the need to do it again.

CHAPTER THREE

THE VICTORIAN HOUSE NEEDED work—the paint on the window casing was peeling, and some areas of the roof bowed. The grass was neatly mowed, and a porch swing with fluffy pillows moved with the breeze. Something about the swing made me think that she often dallied there. Perhaps she liked to read.

"Ready?" Sheriff Wood's voice crackled over the hand-held radio in my car.

I clicked the button on the side. "Hit it."

Several lawmen rushed from the unmarked vehicles along the narrow street. Most converged on the front porch, while a few others rushed around the back. After Mr. Rousseau pleaded not guilty at his arraignment two weeks prior, I set the wheels in motion to crush him. His life was mine to destroy, and I looked forward to watching it crumble.

I climbed out of my car and leaned against it, the sunlight warming my skin and trying to penetrate my dark glasses.

After a swift knock, Sheriff Wood leaned back and kicked the door in. The deputies swarmed inside as if they were looking for the number one man on the most wanted

11

list. In reality, Mr. Rousseau was just a low level schemer and a high level liar.

But I liked the flair of going big, and more than that, I wanted to rattle his daughter's cage. Just the one glimpse of Stella had haunted me. Her soulful eyes, the emotions that roiled beneath her surface, were ingrained in my mind. She was something different. Something wild. While I was a placid lake, nothing daring to touch the treacherous surface, she was a cascading river. Alive where I was dead, making noise while I lay silent.

She was a mystery. One I needed to unravel and devour.

I'd pulled everything on her that I could find—her high school yearbook photo, and a news clipping about her mother's suicide were the highlights. Stella's own suicide attempt intrigued me, and I'd only discovered it after getting her medical records from Dr. Ward, a Vinemont family friend. Her father had found her after she'd slit her wrists. What drove her to it? Him?

Shouting brought me back to the task at hand. Voices rose inside the house, and then quieted. Once satisfied everything was on lockdown, I strolled through the broken front door. A small library was to my left, a sitting room to my right. I continued down the narrow hallway, my shoes silent on the threadbare rug.

"—bust up in here and do whatever you want!"

I turned the corner into a den area where Mr. Rousseau, Stella, and a young man with blond hair stood under the guard of two deputies. The other deputies ransacked Mr. Rousseau's desk. Noise from upstairs told me the deputies were destroying things for fun during their 'search'.

Just as I'd instructed.

"Son, don't make me take you in. Spending the night in a jail cell—"

"You wouldn't dare. My mother is—"

"I don't give a good goddamn who your mother is.

This is an official parish investigation. If you keep interfering, I'll arrest you. Got me?"

"That won't be necessary." I strolled to the deputy as another crash sounded from upstairs.

"You." Mr. Rousseau narrowed his eyes and wrapped his arm around Stella's waist. She wore a white T-shirt and jeans. A simple ensemble that hugged her curves. It would look even better stained with blood or tears, maybe both.

The young man bristled. "Don't look at her."

I met his gaze for a moment. He was muscled with a thick neck. Based on his clothes, he played lacrosse. Based on his muscles, he had a penchant for steroids. I gave him a withering glare and turned to Mr. Rousseau. "I have a warrant. Everything is in order, I assure you."

"Signed by that snake, Judge Montagnet, no doubt." Stella scowled.

A smear of blue paint colored her cheek, and her fingers carried a mix of the same blue and streaks of yellow. I'd visited the small gallery in town and studied the few paintings of hers that hung there. They were dark and brooding. I rather liked them. But her current palette was lighter. I'd work on the colors, pushing her back into darker and darker shades. After all, this was only the first search of many. I intended to turn the screws until Leon Rousseau jumped at every sound and feared I was the monster under his bed.

"Snake, Ms. Rousseau? It isn't wise to impugn a judge's honor, especially one presiding over your father's case."

"We aren't blind, Mr. Vinemont. I saw you in his chambers before the arraignment." Her shoulders moved back, her challenge obvious. My gaze flicked to her hardening nipples. She wasn't wearing a bra. She must have been spending a comfortable day in her house of straw until the big bad wolf came to her door. Now the wolf was inside, and all I wanted to do was eat her up.

"You're impugning my honor as well?" I smirked.

"What do you know about honor?" She threw it back

13

in my face with a quickness that had my blood racing. If I slapped her, would she quiet down or hit me back? I hoped the latter.

"More than the Rousseaus, apparently." I surveyed the room. Sketches and paintings lined the back wall near the tall, narrow windows looking out onto the rear yard. A deputy went to one and ripped it down.

"No." I kept my voice low, but the deputy glanced at me, seemed to shudder, and placed the drawing on a nearby table. He didn't touch any more of the art.

"You can't do this." Mr. Rousseau shook his head and leaned on Stella. He was like a parasite, sucking her life away.

"It's done." I gave Stella one more long, appraising look. Her red hair fell in waves down her shoulders. I wanted to mark her alabaster skin with my teeth.

"I said, stop looking at her." The young man stepped forward.

"Dylan, don't." A warning note laced through her voice. She was smart. One more step and I would drop Dylan on his ass.

"And you are?" I walked past Dylan and studied the closest sketch. I already knew who he was, but I might as well ask to be polite. Mother always wanted me to be polite, though not particularly to trash like the Rousseaus. None of them mattered to me, not even Stella. We were a different species.

"Dylan Devereaux, Leon's stepson."

The sketch appeared to be of a knife, the smooth edge almost glinting on the paper. The handle was a deep mahogany brown, and I smiled at the pool of blood drawn beneath it, some of the drops still on the blade.

"I think we're about done here." Sheriff Wood called as deputies carried boxes of material out to their cars. They'd emptied the entire contents of Mr. Rousseau's desk and taken various other papers they'd found in the house.

"How much for this drawing?" I turned and peered

into Stella's eyes—still fascinating, still full of hatred.

This was only the beginning. Her hatred would build until her other emotions were weak whispers next to how much she wanted to destroy me. I needed to taste her rage, to savor it on my tongue.

"It's not for sale." Her words were even, but I could see the rapid flutter in the vein at her neck. Her heart was racing.

I shot a glance to her father. "Don't be silly. Everything's for sale, right Mr. Rousseau?"

"Get out of here." He scowled.

"While your false disdain is amusing, I'm afraid a jury won't find you quite as believable as your daughter does. So, what's the price?" I kept my gaze on Stella. I wanted her to give in, though I knew she wouldn't.

"I'd rather burn it than sell it to you." Her voice lowered to a hiss as the last of the deputies cleared out.

Her hatred was like a blast of heat on a frigid day. I wanted to strip her flames away, bit by bit, until I reached her core. Once there, would I snuff her fire out, or stoke it until it raged beyond control?

I didn't know the answer. But I knew I wanted her beneath me, my hands on her body, and her blood in my mouth.

"Counsellor?" Sheriff Wood leaned against the doorframe and flipped the strap on his holster off, popped it back on, off, on, off, on.

Stella held my gaze as I strode past.

"Maybe we can continue negotiations the next time I visit."

"You already took everything you wanted." Her father's voice was like a claw in my eardrum.

I turned on my heel and eyed Stella up and down. The line of her legs, the flare of her hips, trim waist, and high, round tits. She shifted uncomfortably under my scrutiny.

I held her defiant gaze. "I'll decide when I've taken everything I want."

CHAPTER FOUR

I LAY IN MY bed and studied Stella's photo. It was already etched into my mind, no need to look at it any longer. But I did.

Someone from my office had snapped it as she left the courthouse after the arraignment. Her hair appeared even more vibrantly red in the sun. Her eyes, though, were sad. I wanted to see them glimmering with tears.

My cock surged at the thought of hurting her. Would she beg? The fire in her eyes told me she wouldn't. Perhaps she would beg me to make it burn, to push her to the edge. The way she'd looked at me during the last search, and the one before that, and the initial one when she'd openly challenged me. *Fuck*.

She wanted to tear me apart. I wanted her to rail against me until she gave in, beaten and defeated. I'd savor every last tear, every cry of pain, and finally, every scream of pleasure.

The violence I'd seen in her eyes made me groan, and my hips surged upward. I slid my hand down to my cock, stroking it slowly as I stared at her photo. Her delicate neck would fit perfectly in my hands. I dropped the picture and clenched my eyes shut, imagining her pale body, the

17

scars on her wrists, the feel of her soft skin. I wanted to bend her to my will, to force her onto her knees and use her—vengeance in her eyes and my cock in her mouth.

I kicked the sheet off. Her mouth was wrapped around me, her smooth tongue weaving along my shaft. I'd tied her hands behind her back, and her ass already bore red welts from my hand and belt.

Licking my lips, I imagined her taste on them as she sucked me, her eyes never wavering from mine. I fisted her hair and pulled her forward until my cock was lodged deep in her throat. Her eyes watered, and I knew she couldn't breathe. I didn't want her to. I held her life in my hands, and I could kill her without a second thought.

Still, her eyes burned with hate, and she tried to fight me off. I didn't let her go, not until her eyes began to glaze and flutter closed. I pulled out and she gasped. I needed to be inside her hot cunt, so I threw her onto the bed. She cried out from the pain of her hands being crushed behind her back, and I savored the sweet sound. I spread her legs and plunged inside her, no warning. I took what I wanted. Her eyes widened with surprise and that delicious spark of agony.

My hand sped, squeezing me just like her pussy would. She fought, trying to buck me off. I only thrust more deeply into her. My balls drew up tight to my body as I clapped my hand over her mouth to muffle her screams.

I sank myself inside her and matched every bit of rage I saw in her eyes with my punishing strokes. She wouldn't break. I had to work harder. I could. I sped my pace, each impact bruising her thighs, her pussy. I reached down and palmed her tit, squeezing mercilessly. Her eyes narrowed, the challenge alive and well. I moved my hand up so it covered both her mouth and nose.

She tried to turn her head, but couldn't escape my strong grip. No air moved inside her body. She fought some more, but I kept taking from her, shoving inside her because I owned her. I didn't let up, suffocating her as I glared down into her rebellious eyes. Her body jerked, still trying to get air.

When she realized I wasn't going to stop, something else lit her gaze, the one thing I'd wanted from her all along. Fear. I came, my cock jolting in my hand as my release spurted onto my stomach. I gasped at how intense the orgasm was, rolling over me and constricting every blood vessel in my body. My cock kicked once more as I relaxed into the bed, my hand still and my heart pounding.

"Fuck." I stared at the ceiling, trying to put all my pieces back into place. *She's no one. No one.* She was nothing to me, other than a body I wanted to use. Nothing.

This time she sat on the swing reading when the cruisers rolled up to the house. She glanced up, shook her head, then went back to her book. The deputies got out and strolled up the front porch. They flashed a warrant. She ignored it.

She said something I couldn't hear and waved at the door. Ten men entered the house. I'd asked them to get even rowdier than the last couple of times. More than a few items would be destroyed during this 'search' I smirked and continued to stare at her. A hot summer breeze rustled the first of the fallen leaves on the lawns nearby. Fall was almost here, and her father's trial was set for the following week.

Two days of testimony and he'd be convicted. There was no other option for a parish jury, especially given the dirt I had on the old man. Then sentencing. I'd have him sent to the nastiest pen in the state. His suffering would only weaken her, make her ripe for the taking.

She continued perusing her book, only turning her head to the side a couple of times—likely when she heard something break inside. I was a little disappointed she didn't get up to investigate or make a scene, but I'd rather keep my eyes on her anyway. I knew it bothered her, so it was the best of both worlds.

I slid my gaze down her v-neck shirt—the bare swell of her breasts just visible. Her athletic shorts showed plenty of leg, and I admired the way her calves tapered to narrow ankles. I wanted to knot rope around them and spread them wide. A flogger to the pussy would shake any woman's resolve, even Stella's.

The breeze picked up again and splayed tendrils of her hair across her face. She brushed them out of the way and stretched. Her back arched. My cock swelled to a painful degree. She brought her arms back down and glanced out to the road. She froze, her eyes locked with mine.

She cocked her head to the side again, listening to the sounds inside the house, and scowled. The deputies must have been following my instructions with verve. Tossing her book to the side, she rose, her eyes never leaving me as she strode down the front walk, her bare feet silent on the cracked concrete.

I couldn't stop the smirk that turned my lip at the corner. She wanted a confrontation. I would give it to her. Rolling my passenger window down, I waited. She arrived and bent over. I saw her simple white bra. I could rip it off in two seconds, and I wanted to. When I caught her lilac scent, my cock went from hard to painfully hard. My jacket hid it. She held my gaze, that fire inside her burning brighter by the second.

"Pleased with yourself?" Even when she was harsh, her voice still had a melodic quality.

"I'm sorry, Ms. Rousseau. I don't quite take your meaning." My mask was in place—I was the parish prosecutor, a public servant to the core. Everything I did was in the name of the law.

"There is nothing here. There hasn't been anything here since the first time you came. Why are you doing this?" She peered at me, but she didn't see me. Just my mask.

"I have to make sure every piece of evidence is collected. After all, you wouldn't want me to miss the one document or item that could exonerate your father, would you? I have to be thorough."

She dug her nails into the trim along the window sill. "You don't fool me for a second. You just like to torment him. That's all you're doing."

"I'm only doing the job I was elected to do. Keeping the parish safe from fraudulent operators like your father."

"You're lying."

Always. "I'm sorry to hear you think so. I truly am."

"We'll see at the trial. No one will believe your lies then."

I tsked at her and shook my head. "You think he'll win, don't you?" I laughed. "Foolish. Then again, I never took you as particularly clever. Not like he is."

"Insult me all you like, but the truth will come out. My father will be found innocent, because that's what he is."

She actually believed her father's lies. Why was it so hard for her to believe mine?

"We'll see. Now, I have much more important affairs to tend to than your diatribes. If you'll excuse me." I cranked the car.

She didn't move, her green gaze still taking in my mask. There were no cracks in it, nowhere she could see inside. I'd crafted it so well that people had no idea it was actually a mask to begin with.

"I see you." She spoke through gritted teeth.

"That makes sense as I'm sitting right in front of you in broad daylight." The hackles on the back of my neck rose as she stared harder, her eyes glinting.

"No. I see the real you. Don't think for a second that you're fooling me. It may work on everyone else. But I see what you really are." She pulled her hands away. "And you disgust me."

21

"If that was some sort of threat, it fell flat, Ms. Rousseau. Maybe work on your inflection and try again next time. I'll attempt to act sufficiently frightened." I turned the wheel.

She backed away as I hit the gas and cruised down the street. I stared at her in my rearview mirror, her arms crossed over her chest and her mouth drawn down in a scowl.

I didn't want to leave. What I'd wanted to do was grip her shirt and yank her into the car. Kidnapping her in broad daylight wasn't an option, unfortunately. But if I had, how long would it take before she screamed? Before true fear overcame the steel lining her spine?

I didn't know, but I wanted to find out.

CHAPTER FIVE

"I HAVE NO FURTHER questions." Mr. Rousseau's attorney sat down. The fool had put Mr. Rousseau on the witness stand when he should have remained silent.

I cracked my knuckles, and Judge Montagnet turned away from the jury to hide his grin. This would be fun.

The gallery was filled with Mr. Rousseau's victims, each one of them having already testified in the State's case in chief. The jury had listened to every word, every syllable about what a dirty schemer Mr. Rousseau was.

Stella sat behind her father, the circles under her eyes growing darker with each passing day. We'd just come back from lunch, and I was more than ready to take my time with her father, squeeze out every last lie and hold it up for the jury—and Stella—to see.

I couldn't help myself. I shot a glance at her over my shoulder as I rose and buttoned my suit coat. She kept her gaze on her father. Good.

"I have a few questions, if you don't mind, Your Honor."

"You may examine the witness." Montagnet had composed himself and leaned back in his chair, ready for the show.

I strode forward and positioned myself directly in front of the jury. Leon Rousseau was on trial, but I was the star of the show.

I clutched my hands in front of me, humbleness in every calculated movement. "Mr. Rousseau, I'm Sinclair Vinemont, the parish prosecutor. We've met before—"

"I know who you are." His snarl, though understandable, did not play well to the jury. Two of the ladies on the back row shifted uncomfortably in their seats.

"You remember meeting Mrs. Caldwell?" I motioned to the elderly woman with the tennis balls attached to her walker. She sat in the front row, her aged face in a permanent frown.

Mr. Rousseau, sweat beading along his upper lip, nodded. "Yes."

"You told her to invest in Mirabella, a tenants-in-common product?"

"Yes."

I turned to the jury, affecting a teaching tone. "Tenants-in-common means that several investors go in together to buy a property, one that is usually fully leased and provides steady income via rent payments and increase in value in the property market. Is that correct, Mr. Rousseau?"

"Yes."

"Mirabella was a good investment for Mrs. Caldwell?"

"Yes." His tone turned warier with each affirmative response.

"It would provide steady income to pay her living expenses?"

"Yes."

"Especially when the housing market is on an upswing, like now?"

"Yes."

"So." I turned to the jury. "It was a highly suitable and wise investment?"

"Yes."

"But you didn't invest her money into Mirabella, did you, Mr. Rousseau?"

He swallowed hard and looked away.

"Mr. Rousseau, did you invest her money into Mirabella?"

"I-I…"

"It's a simple yes or no answer. Which is it?"

His watery eyes fell. "No."

"You told her you did?"

"Yes."

"But you actually put that money into another account?"

"Yes."

"An interest-bearing account with your name on it?"

"Yes, but I was going to transfer her investment—"

"You never put her money in any other investment, did you?"

"No, but I was going to." He talked quickly. "I was waiting until the market bounce—"

"Mrs. Caldwell never received a dime of interest?"

"No. But if you'd just let me explain. She'd been in a series of annuities that actually depleted her principal at a far faster rate. I would have transferred her money over into the Mirabella accounts once I received all of her principal from the annuity companies, but you froze my accounts before I had the chance."

"I see." I nodded as if I agreed with his assessment. "So, you were trying to help Mrs. Caldwell?"

"Yes." He surveyed the jurors, trying to make eye contact with each one.

"Are you aware of a rule for financial advisors, like yourself, that states any commingling of funds results in a total disbarment?"

"Yes, but—"

"And isn't it true that you were barred from working as a financial advisor by the financial regulatory agency three months ago?"

He turned his gaze toward me. "Because of you. Because you testified to all these lies about me. I did nothing wrong."

"Nothing wrong? Didn't you just admit to putting Mrs. Caldwell's money into your personal account?"

"Yes, but—"

"Do you remember the first time you met Mr. Calgary?" I pointed to an elderly man in a wheelchair who glared at Mr. Rousseau.

Mrs. Caldwell, Mr. Calgary, Mrs. Green, Mr. Bradley, Mr. Hess, Mr. Graves, Mrs. Oppen, Mr. Travis—I went through each elderly victim, each transaction, each instance of misappropriation. Mr. Rousseau had an excuse each time I pointed out that their funds always wound up in his personal accounts. By the end of my cross examination, several of the jurors leaned back with their arms crossed. They didn't believe him, were repulsed by him, just like I was.

When I finished, and Mr. Rousseau's excuses finally died out, I turned to the judge. "The State rests, Your Honor, but we would move for a judgment of guilt as a matter of law, given Mr. Rousseau's own testimony here today."

"Mr. Rousseau, you may step down." Judge Montagnet looked to Mr. Rousseau's counsel table. "You have anything to say about that?"

The mediocre attorney stood and bumbled with his file. "I, uh, I object and move for a judgment of acquittal."

"Both motions denied. I'll let the jury have it." He peered at his wrist watch.

"It's quarter to four, Judge."

"Thank you, Counsellor Vinemont." He shook his head. "These old eyes can't quite see how they used to. I'll go ahead and charge the jury and let them begin deliberations."

I strode to my table, giving Stella a long look as I walked. She tried to school her features, but it didn't work.

Venom, rage, and pain were writ large across her pale face. I savored every bit of emotion that skittered off her like sparks.

The judge instructed the jury concerning the elements of each charge and how they should go about making their decision. Then he sent them to deliberate. As soon as the last juror left the room, Stella rushed through the swinging wooden door and hugged her father. Dylan followed and put his meaty hand on Stella's back.

I sized him up again. He was big, but I'd killed bigger with nothing more than my bare hands. The way he touched her set something off inside me. I didn't know what. It was as if a slimy eel swirled in my stomach. It mixed with the one feeling I could recognize with ease— hatred.

"Come on, Dad. Let's get some air."

I smiled. "Yes, take him outside while you still can. He won't be a free man for much longer." The elderly people seated behind me mumbled and grunted in agreement.

Stella whirled and took a step toward me. Her fine hands were fisted, and I could sense how badly she wanted to hurt me. My cold blood heated a degree or two, and a flash of me yanking up her skirt and bending her over the counsel table went straight to my cock.

Taking a deep breath, she un-balled her fists and stretched her paint-stained fingers out straight. She must have thought better of going toe-to-toe with me. Too bad. She turned and took her father's elbow. Dylan sneered as he walked past, but I didn't give him the satisfaction of even looking in his direction.

I kept the image of Stella in my mind, relishing the way her hate kept me warm.

The jury returned in less than an hour.

They filed in one by one, and the foreman handed the judge their verdict. The jurors wouldn't meet Mr. Rousseau's eyes. Their verdict couldn't have been more obvious.

"All rise." The bailiff's voice brought the courtroom to its feet as Judge Montagnet skimmed down the verdict form, his mouth moving with silent words.

"I think everything is in order here." The judge handed the verdict form back to the foreman, who returned to the jury box. "Has the jury reached a verdict?"

"We have, Your Honor," the foreman responded.

"Please read it aloud."

The foreman cleared his throat and shot a quick look to Mr. Rousseau. "We, the jury, find Leon Rousseau guilty on all counts."

Sighs and murmurs of approval erupted from the gallery. Mr. Rousseau sank into his chair, and Stella rushed up and put her hand on his shoulder.

"Daddy, it'll be okay. It'll be okay." Her fervent whisper was a lie. I would make sure of that.

"Would you like me to poll the jury?" Judge Montagnet asked.

"Not for the State, Your Honor." I buttoned my suit jacket and stepped around the counsel table.

"Defense?"

"No, Your Honor."

He turned to the jury. "In that case, you all are free to go. Thank you for your service." Judge Montagnet banged his gavel, and the crowd at my back grew loud with chatter.

The jurors filed out of the box. I shook each one's hand as they passed and assured them they'd done the right thing. They smiled and nodded, because I was telling them exactly what they wanted to hear.

Once I'd shaken all their hands, I walked into the gallery and received pats on the back and 'bless you's' from the teary victims. I figured I'd have to burn this suit after all the touching. These people disgusted me only slightly less than Mr. Rousseau, but I slapped on what I knew was a pleasant smile and accepted their congratulations and grimy thanks.

The victims eventually cleared out of the gallery and headed toward the courthouse elevator. The room emptied until only the defendant, Stella, Dylan, and I remained.

Stella hadn't shed a tear even as her father turned into a blubbering mess. Dylan tried to comfort him with nonsense like 'appeal' and 'they can't do this'. Mr. Rousseau would be long dead before his appeal was ever heard.

I should have left. Then again, I'd never been one to pass up a final twist of the knife. I walked around the table to face all three of them.

"I'll have Judge Montagnet bump your sentencing up to next week. That way you can start serving your time as soon as possible. It'll give you a better chance of getting out before you die. Though, sorry to say, that is still quite unlikely."

Mr. Rousseau's blubbering increased.

"Do you lack even a shred of decency?" Stella's accusation missed the mark, given I had quite a bit more decency than anyone on her side of the table.

"I was only trying to be helpful." I smirked.

She straightened her back, the dark gray of her skirt suit giving her eyes a steely quality. "You're a bully. A menace parading as a saint. I see right through you."

"As you keep telling me. But, I don't think the jury had the same vision."

"Sin?" Judge Montagnet called through the door to his chambers.

Stella's mouth compressed into a thin line, and Dylan edged closer to her.

"Coming, Judge," I called. "I'll see you all next week. Don't be late, Mr. Rousseau. You're still out on bond for

29

now. Just keep in mind that I'll have Sheriff Wood drag you up here if I have to." I gave Stella a congenial smile and turned on my heel, walking straight back to the judge's chambers.

"I see you." Her voice wafted to my ears as the door swung closed behind me.

CHAPTER SIX

"CAN I COME?" TEDDY plopped down on my bed.

I smoothed my button-down shirt, though it had already been ironed to crisp perfection. "No."

"Why not?" He tossed a baseball in the air and caught it. Tossed it again, missed it, and it hit himself in the nose.

I laughed as he cursed and rolled back and forth on my bed. "Good one, Ted."

If there was one bright spot in my dark existence, it was my youngest brother. Somehow, my fucked up family hadn't managed to erase whatever spark he kept inside. Did I ever have a spark?

"Shut up." He pinched his nose and winced, his voice coming out as a nasal whine. "Why can't I go?"

"Because you weren't invited. Besides, it's at Cal's house."

He grimaced. "Never mind. I'm glad I wasn't invited."

"Was I invited?" Lucius strode in and took the ball from Teddy.

"That's mine."

"Not anymore." Lucius threw it up and caught it right above Teddy's crotch.

"Not cool, man." Teddy scowled.

"No, what wouldn't have been cool is if I hadn't caught it."

"You two are dicks. I'm going to my room." Teddy stood and gingerly touched his nose.

"You're still pretty. Get over it." Lucius took Teddy's spot on my bed.

"I'll see you when I get back, Ted. Okay?" I smiled at him in the mirror. I couldn't tell if I was faking it or not.

He returned it, so perhaps it had been genuine after all. "Yeah. See you later."

"Don't worry, little bro." Lucius grinned. "I'll be here to take care of you, wipe your ass, rub on the baby lotion, hold your dick when you piss—all that." Teddy flipped him off and walked down the hall.

"You shouldn't taunt him so much." I threaded my tie around my neck and began to knot it.

"He needs to toughen up if he wants to hang with us."

"I hope that he won't have to hang with us. Medical school will get him out of here. Away from all this, from us."

"What's so bad about us?" He tossed the ball up and caught it again.

"He isn't..." My fingers hesitated on my tie. "He doesn't deserve this life."

Lucius shrugged. "I think you're underestimating him."

"I'm not saying it's a bad thing." I finished my tie and checked it. The knot was perfect, the deep blue of the tie setting off the lighter hue of my shirt. "I want him to stay the way he is. I don't want him to turn into..."

"You?" Lucius finished for me.

I cocked my head at him in the mirror. "There are worse things he could be. *You*, for instance."

"He should be so lucky."

I'd showered and shaved. My dark hair was smoothed down. Nothing was out of place. Perfection was my favorite form of control.

"You think he'll ever man up and get inked?" he asked.

"It doesn't matter either way. He's a Vinemont with or without the crest on his skin."

"I think he will. All the girls in Baton Rouge will be on his dick if he shows up with the vines on his arms."

I plucked my cuff links from the small box on top of my dresser. "Maybe."

"Fuck, no 'maybe' about it. Chicks love tats. I wouldn't mind trolling sorority row myself. Get some fresh pussy."

"They might be interested in him, but I've noticed him giving the new cook more than a few looks."

"You going to let him hit that?"

"No." I raised an eyebrow at him in the mirror as he continued tossing the baseball. "You know that sort of fraternization isn't allowed. She's a peasant. He's a Vinemont."

"But, come on, you've fucked chicks who aren't top stock."

Once my sleeves were perfected, I slid my arms into the jacket. "Not ones who are servants in my house. No."

"I don't think it would be so terrible if he got his dick wet with her. That's all I'm saying."

"You'd be wrong, as usual." I chose a pair of black oxfords and laced them while pondering what was in store for me at Cal's house.

An invitation to the Oakman Estate wasn't something to be taken lightly. Cal Oakman, as Sovereign, controlled too much, had too many allies, and had grown more dangerous each year of his reign. I didn't know what the party was for, but I was certain it couldn't be a good thing. Over the past ten years, he'd left the Vinemonts alone most of the time, only sending word when he decided to increase his cut of our family's sugar business.

We were living quietly under his thumb until a week ago when his invitation arrived, the wax seal imprinted with the all-too-familiar oak. Dread had spread across my mind as I'd opened the letter. A dinner at Cal Oakman's house on the eve of the Acquisition trials—nothing good could come of it. I straightened and turned to leave my room.

"You sure I can't come?"

"I'm sure."

Lucius followed me into the hall and down the front stairs. "You have any idea what he wants?"

"The same thing he always wants. Too much."

"Do you think…" Lucius hesitated on the bottom step as Farns, our butler, opened the front door for me.

I stopped and let Lucius ask. The same question had been haunting me from the moment the invitation arrived.

"Do you think it'll be us this year?" The anticipation in his voice told me he was thinking about it like a business arrangement. Being chosen could lead to wealth and, obviously, position. But there was another side—a much darker side—to it all. One he didn't know about.

"I'm about to find out." I squared my shoulders and walked out into the night.

CHAPTER SEVEN

ABOUT TWENTY CARS LINED the drive to the overdone Oakman estate. Modelled on Versailles, but even gaudier, it dominated the acres of perfectly-mowed lawn surrounding it. The windows sparkled into the gloom, and a handful of guests climbed the stairs to the front entrance.

Luke, my driver, pulled to the front. The valet opened my door, and I stepped out into the muggy southern heat. I made quick work of the stairs and entered the sprawling chateau. Crystal chandeliers hung in a line down the main hallway as party guests broke into cliques.

"Sinclair, my man!" Cal strode up and shook my hand. "Welcome, welcome. So glad you could make it."

As if I had any choice in the matter. Turning down an invitation from the Sovereign would result in a myriad of consequences that I didn't even want to contemplate.

"Thanks for having me." I smiled at him as a tall, willowy redhead in a light blue dress walked up and linked her arm in his.

"Gretchen, my love, where have you been?" Cal slid his hand down to her ass.

She winced.

"Still sore from our earlier fun, sweetheart?" He

slapped her ass and she bit her lip, wetness brimming in her glassy eyes. "That's what I like to see." He watched as a tear rolled down her overpainted cheek. "Sin, head on down to the dining room. We're about to start."

"Sounds good." I turned and heard another slap coupled with a pained squeal. Cal had always been a sadist. The redhead didn't realize it, but she was getting off easy. He was capable of much, much worse.

Another slap and another cry followed me down the long hallway. I smiled whenever it seemed appropriate and shook hands with other party guests.

"They invited the Vinemonts? And here I was thinking this was going to be a classy affair." Red Witherington scowled at me from his group of chuckling friends.

"Sad to see that the beating I gave you last spring didn't temper your bad manners any." I smirked as his face fell. "But I'm always up to try again."

"You're lucky we're at Cal's place." He stepped toward me. "Anywhere else, I'd take you the fuck out."

I laughed. "You've always been such an entertainer. I'll tell your sister about this little show tonight once she's done calling me daddy. She's a real screamer. Did you know—"

"Fucking prick!" He lunged at me, but one of his friends held him back. Lucky for Red.

I remained still, even as he tried to surge forward and attack. "See you at dinner, Red. I hope you'll be on your best behavior in front of the Sovereign."

"Motherfucker!"

"Maybe after your sister, sure." I strode past him as his friends tried to talk him down.

I was more than happy to step outside and beat Red unconscious, but I had more pressing matters. Returning greetings, I continued down the hall.

Only select families of the Louisiana elite were in attendance, though I couldn't tell what the significance of the guest list was. There were other sugar producers, yes, but also bankers, politicians, jewelers, textile manufacturers, and a host of others.

Even without any hints from the assemblage, the timing couldn't be missed. We were only a week away from the start of the Acquisition. The rumor was that Cal had already chosen and met with the competitors. Perhaps this was simply a party to congratulate them. The unease in the pit of my stomach said otherwise.

My discomfort grew with each step toward the dining room. A few guests were already inside, chatting among themselves.

"Sin." Sophia glided over, her silvery dress shimmering in the light. "Haven't seen you in a while. Where's Lucius?"

I smiled down into her dark eyes. "He wasn't invited. Besides, am I not enough?"

She let her eyes travel down my body and then back up. "You're more than enough. I haven't seen you for a while, though. How's the public servant routine going?"

"Fine. I have to deal with the rabble far too much for my tastes, but I'll live. How about in-house counsel work? Still enjoying it?"

She wrinkled her perfect nose. "I would hate to have to deal with the lower classes on a daily basis. I don't know how you manage it." She flipped her smooth dark hair over her bare shoulder, the skin smooth and tan. "In-house work is much more enjoyable, though time consuming. I still manage to travel quite a—"

Cal's voice boomed down the hall. "Let's get started, everyone."

"I'll see you around." She gave me a silky smile before retreating toward the other end of the table.

I chose a seat near the far end, the better to observe Cal and the other guests. He walked in, his chest puffed out and his arms spread wide. "Welcome, welcome. Take your seats." Striding to the head of the table, he motioned for everyone to sit.

Cordelia Shaw sat on my right, Bob Eagleton on my left. We exchanged pleasantries as the servers brought bread and salad to the table.

"What do you think we're here for?" Cordelia whispered through her crimson lips. She was the eldest Shaw, her blond hair and bright blue eyes marking her as one of the most attractive women at the table.

"No idea." I speared a piece of lettuce. "But the ball is next week."

She shuddered at my elbow, her pert breast rubbing against me through her thin dress. "I hope it's not me."

I shared her sentiment on most levels, but there was one part of me that wanted to take the crown and all the perks that came with it. Ruling over the nobility would bring me wealth and power beyond anything I could imagine. I considered the row of people, their jewels sparkling, their very demeanors soaked in luxury and privilege. To rule them would be an engaging game, one that would keep me satisfied for the next decade. But the specter of my mother warned me away from any such ambition—her broken mind was a powerful blow against competing in the Acquisition trials.

"Think it'll be you?" she whispered and took a sip of her wine.

I maintained my nonchalant air as I carefully buttered my bread. "I heard he'd already chosen."

She shook her head, her large diamond earring wobbling. "That's just a rumor. I think—I think this is it."

"We'll see."

Talk continued around us as the first course was cleared away, and the servers brought out the entrées. Bob spilled his wine halfway through the main course and proceeded to blame the staff for his ruined shirt and suit. His round belly took the brunt of the damage, a wine stain spreading across the taut fabric like blood. Despite his setback, he made quick work of his fillet, likely never even tasting the savory notes of rosemary and garlic infused into the meat.

Once we reached the end of the entrées, Cal stood. The table chatter ceased immediately.

"Bring the dessert."

A wave of servers entered, carrying petite chocolate cakes atop thin bars of gold. My stomach lurched. I recognized the golden 'plates'. They were invitations to the Acquisition Ball. I'd seen a similar one ten years prior, but I didn't attend the ball or any of the trials. This year, with Cal in charge, would be different. He apparently wanted to kick off the trials with a bang.

A server set one of the cakes in front of me, the chocolate concoction in the form of a small mound with a dimple in the center.

Cal clapped his hands, the sound like a shot. "As you all know, the Acquisition Ball will be held here next Friday. The rest of the invitations are, even as we sit here, going out across the South—and the country, for that matter— to attendees. It's going to be an amazing year." He grinned and stroked his hand down his tie. "You will all remember this Acquisition as the most momentous one of your lifetimes. I guarantee it."

A smattering of polite applause rippled around the room.

"Stop, stop. You flatter me." His grin grew even wider, his too-white teeth splitting his face into halves. "But there's one more thing I need to do before we get started. I have to pick the competitors."

The room was so silent that it seemed most of its occupants were holding their breaths.

"Before you, sits a decadent dessert." Cal waved down the table.

I eyed the innocuous cake. Was something rotten inside?

"It's tasty. I may have sampled one before dinner." He rubbed his stomach for emphasis. "As you all know, I love surprises. So, my three chosen Acquirers will have a little something different inside their cakes. You'll know it when you see it, ladies and gents."

He raised his glass. "Pick up your spoons and dig in."

The guests hesitated, some of them clenching their eyes shut to avoid finding out. I took my spoon and perched it over the smooth cake, trying to discern if it would blow up in my face or simply ooze into a chocolaty mess.

"Thank God." Cordelia had cut into her cake. Dark chocolate cascaded from it, and she split it all the way open just to be sure. It was just a dessert, nothing more. She dropped her spoon as if it had burned her. Quiet sighs of relief rose from the table.

"Oh." Bob spit into his napkin. "This tastes horrible."

His golden plate was covered with crimson and the distinct scent of copper rose from the cake's warm interior.

"It's blood."

He shrugged and wiped the red from his lips. Disgusting.

A whoop sounded from the end of the table near Cal. It was Red Witherington. "Fuck yeah!" He laughed.

Cal grinned at him and then glanced around the table. When his eyes landed on me and stayed, the hairs at the back of my neck stood on end.

"One more." He didn't look away. Others caught on and began to stare, waiting for the reveal.

There was no way out, no way to stop the inevitable. I eased the spoon into the cake. It slid easily. No filling escaped as the edge of the spoon tapped against the gold beneath. I twisted the spoon slightly. A stream of blood flowed around the silver and pooled on the gold.

It sank into the grooves of the invitation and put the letters in sharp relief. There was no mistaking the words that had been cut into the golden surface, now darkened with crimson. Sinclair Vinemont, Acquirer.

CHAPTER EIGHT

I STARED AT THE ceiling. I'd been doing it for the past few nights—ever since Cal's dinner. The rules played over and over in my mind as I traced the corners of the room with my gaze. Three Acquirers, one victor. Winning would cement the Vinemonts at the top of society. Wealth, privilege, and the freedom to live our lives in any way we chose.

Losing. I closed my eyes. I wouldn't think about losing. Tossing the sheet off, I stood and strode to the shower. Mr. Rousseau's sentencing was set to start in two hours.

I left the bathroom light off, soaking up the darkness as the warm liquid cascaded down my body. In the inky black of the bathroom, I couldn't tell if it was water or something worse.

Red hair, green eyes, fair skin—Stella floated along the river of blood that ran through my mind. I'd wanted her for myself. I'd wanted to claim her on my own terms, to master her and break her my way. The fire that burned inside her lured me closer because I wanted so badly to feel the burn. But the game was no longer my own. I'd wanted her before. Now, I needed her.

Would the fire that burned inside her be enough to see

her through the trials?

I soaped up and rinsed off, ready to put my plans into motion. After I shaved and dressed, I headed into town. Specifically, to Judge Montagnet's chambers. He waited inside, his law clerk nude and on all fours on the floor. A thin trickle of blood ran down the young man's thigh, and I ignored his tears as I sank down onto the judge's sofa. He puffed on a cigar and blew the smoke into the sniffling clerk's face.

"Got my morning started off right." Montagnet smiled. "Get dressed and get out." He kicked the clerk, who hurriedly dressed and escaped into the adjoining office.

"I heard about Cal's selections." He took a hard drag on the cigar, the tip flaming orange.

I nodded and smoothed my hands along my thighs. "Yes."

"You picked who you're going to acquire?"

"Yes." I pulled a sheaf of paper from my pocket and handed it to him.

He glanced it over and smiled. "Smart boy." He rose and shuffled to his desk. Drawing out a fountain pen, he signed the document with a flourish, then folded it up. He used his lighter to heat a small nub of wax, pressed it to the paper, and then affixed his seal to it. "All done here." He handed it back.

I blew on the seal. He watched me and licked his lips.

Once satisfied it was cooled, I placed it in my pocket next to its counterparts.

He sank back down and rubbed his knees. "Damn, these floors grow harder the older I get."

I nodded in empty agreement despite my revulsion.

He zipped his robe all the way up, his appearance of fairness complete. "I guess we'd better hop to it. Time for the sentencing to start." After lurching to his feet, he lumbered to the door leading to the courtroom. He peeked over his shoulder, his eyebrows high. "So, *Counsellor*, you think you'll get her?"

I stood and followed him through the door, my mask firmly in place. "I know I will."

Available Now

CHAPTER ONE
SINCLAIR

IN THE HEART OF every man is a darkness. Primal. Instinctive.

At its most basic, it's a desirous nature—one that covets, demands, takes. Most men brick it up behind a wall of self-control. They invest time and effort in maintaining the separation. These men, good men, control the darkness until it withers away and becomes nothing more than a shadow haunting their innermost thoughts. Something easily forgotten, dismissed, erased.

I've never been a good man.

My darkness is neither restrained nor buried. It lives right at the surface. The only thing that hides it is my mask.

My mask is the law, the light, the pursuit of justice. It is forthright and airy. It is the appearance of righteousness in a fallen world.

The mask I wear is purely the act of a predator. Theater. Pageantry. Deceptive and lethal. It allows me to get close, and closer still, until it is time to strike.

I stalk so near that my prey can feel the tickle of my breath, the coldness of my heart, the depth of my depravity. Only a whisper separates me from what I desire.

Then the mask falls away, and all my victim sees is darkness.

CHAPTER TWO
STELLA

THE DISTRICT ATTORNEY SAT completely still at the dark, polished table across the courtroom. My father sat in front of me at an identical table, but he was full of nervous energy. He shifted, ran a hand through his silver hair, and leaned over to whisper to his attorney.

I clasped my hands in my lap until the ring on my index finger dug into my flesh. This was the last chance my father had for freedom, the last day he would be able to throw himself on the mercy of the court. My gaze wandered back to the district attorney, the one who had my father arrested. Investigators scrutinized every last cent the old man ever invested or borrowed. And, just like that, my world became a smoldering heap of ashes. All because of one man.

Sinclair Vinemont was unmoving, like a spider poised on a web, waiting for the slightest sensation of movement from a hapless moth. My father was the moth, and Vinemont was about to destroy him. The investigation and prosecution had been the careful work of a master. Vinemont had woven the cocoon tighter and tighter until my father was caught from all sides. He had nowhere to

47

run, nowhere to try and hide from Vinemont's poison. Dad was being systematically dismantled by the silent monster in a perfect suit.

I wanted to crumble. I couldn't. Dad needed me. No matter the long list of allegations and the even longer list of evidence against him, he was my father. He had always been there for me. Always protected me, stood by me, and encouraged me. Even after what my mother had done. Even after what I had done.

I would not leave his side. He was staring down a hefty prison sentence. Even if the worst happened, I would visit him, call him, write him, and keep him company until the day he got out. I owed him that, and much more.

I stared at Vinemont so hard I hoped he would burst into flames from the sheer heat of my hatred. I'd wished for his demise for so long it had become like second nature to me. I hated him, hated every slick word from his mouth, every breath he took. Vinemont's downfall was stuck on replay in my mind. As I glared at his back, he remained tranquil, completely at ease despite my father coming apart with worry at the table next to him.

I forced myself to drop my gaze, lest anyone see me glaring at him with embittered rage. I couldn't bear for my father to suffer any further torment, especially not if it was based on any of my actions. My hands were pale in my lap, a white contrast to my dark pinstriped skirt. I took a deep breath and settled myself. It would do no good for me to fall apart now. Not in the face of my father's sentencing. I let out my breath slowly and looked up.

Something was different. I darted my gaze to the side. Sinclair Vinemont sat just as still, but now his eyes were trained on me. His gaze pierced me, as if he were seeing more than my exterior. I refused to turn away and, instead, gave him a matching stare full of righteous anger. We were locked in a battle, though not a word was said and no one threw a punch. I wouldn't look away. I wouldn't let him win even more than he already had. I perused his appearance more fully than I had ever dared. He would have been handsome—dark hair, blue eyes, and a strong jaw. He was tall, broad, fit. The perfect man except for the ice I knew coated his heart.

The internet had told me everything I needed to know about him. Single, old money, career in public service, and at twenty-nine years old, he was the youngest district attorney in parish history. The only thing I didn't know about him was why he would dare look at me, why he thought he had any right to pin me with his gaze after he'd ruined my life. I wanted to spit in his face, claw his eyes, and make him hurt the same way he'd hurt my father and me.

The door at the front of the courtroom opened and the judge entered, a stark, elderly man in black robes. Vinemont finally turned away, vanquished for the time being. Everyone in the courtroom stood. The judge shuffled to his seat behind a high wall of wood and state insignias, far above the spectators and lawyers.

"Be seated." Despite his apparent age, his voice boomed, echoing off the dusty shutters and up into the gallery above. "Counsellor Vinemont..." He trailed off, sorting through the papers on his desk.

My father sank into his chair and turned to grant me a thin smile. I tried to smile back to give him some sort of comfort, but it was too late. He'd already faced forward, watching the judge. I willed the judge to let my father go, to suspend his sentence, to do anything except take him away from me. I had no one else. No mother. No one except Dylan, and I refused to rely on him for anything.

Vinemont stood and fastened the top button of his suit coat before stepping from behind the table. He was tall, and like so many dangerous things, effortlessly beautiful.

The bespectacled, bearded judge was still rifling through sheets upon sheets of documents when Vinemont spoke.

"Judge Montagnet, I have several victims lined up to

speak against Mr. Rousseau." His deep Southern drawl was an affront to my ears. Even so, words spilled off his tongue with ease. He could charm the devil himself. As far as I was concerned, Sinclair Vinemont *was* the devil.

I wished we'd never left New York, never travelled to this backwoods bayou full of snakes. Vinemont condemned my father with airy ease every chance he got. No one spoke against him. No one countered his venomous lies other than the ham-handed defense attorney my father hired. So many of the people we'd met in this town were good, forthright souls—or so I'd thought. They weren't here. They didn't sit on my father's side to give him support against Vinemont's false charges. They hadn't come to testify that my father's sentence should be reduced or that he should be granted mercy. It was only me and rows upon rows of empty, cold pews. We were alone.

On Vinemont's side of the courtroom, two rows full of people, maybe twenty in all, sat and glared at Dad and me. Most of them were elderly men and women who had invested with my father. They blamed him for losing their money when all he did was invest as they requested. He had no control over the market, or the crashes, or the resulting instability. My father wasn't the monster Vinemont had made him out to be.

One of the women, gray and wrinkly, met my gaze and made the sign of the evil eye. I only knew what it was because she'd done it before, the last time I'd seen her in court during my father's trial. I'd looked it up and realized she was cursing me. With each movement of her hand, she was willing destruction down on my head. I looked away, back to the true reason for my father's disgrace and my desperation. Sinclair Vinemont.

The judge nodded. "Bring up your first witness, Counsellor."

I steeled myself as one by one, the alleged victims walked, limped, or wheeled past me to testify against my father. Their tears should have moved me, their tales of trust broken and fortunes lost should have forced some shred of empathy from my heart. All I felt was anger. Anger at them for getting my father into this mess. More than that, anger at Vinemont as he stood and patted the 'victims' on the shoulder or the arm and gave out hugs like he was running for office. Every so often I could have sworn he leered back at me, some sort of smug satisfaction on his hard face.

The day droned on with story after story. With each witness, Dad slumped down farther in his chair, as if trying to melt away into the floor. I wanted to put my hand on his shoulder, tell him things could be fixed. Instead, I sat like a statue and listened.

The accusations stung me like a swarm of hornets. After the sixth or seventh witness, I went numb from their venom. Despite the breadth of the charges, I did not doubt my father. Not for a moment. Vinemont had done all this to ensure his re-election or for some other, similarly vile purpose.

When the last witness finally turned her walker around and shuffled back to her seat, the silence became a separate presence. Heavy, ominous, and draining, like a specter haunting the empty spaces of the room. My father remained hunched forward, his head bowed.

"Well, judge, I think you've heard enough." Vinemont held his hands out beside him, the show at an end.

"I have. I'm going to need the evening to think on the sentence." He glanced around the courtroom, his impassive gaze stopping on me for a moment longer than anyone else. "I'll have my verdict in the morning."

Vinemont turned to the judge and gave him a slight nod. Judge Montagnet returned the nod and then banged his gavel. "Court is adjourned."

"Just let me make you feel better." Dylan leaned over me, pushing me sideways onto the ancient leather sofa in my father's library.

"I can't do this right now." I tried to push him off but he pressed harder, overcoming my balance so I fell on my back beneath him.

He put his mouth to my neck, sucking my skin between his teeth. He was large and well-muscled thanks to endless lacrosse and rowing. He crushed me and constricted my chest.

"Please, Dylan." I gasped. I should have been afraid. I wasn't. I was still dazed from the courthouse. Dylan was just adding to the long line of disappointments I'd suffered over the past six months.

He pushed his knee between my legs.

"I can make it all go away for you," he murmured against me. "Just let me make you feel good for a minute. You need a break."

He forced his hand up my skirt.

"Stella? Where are you?" My father's voice calling my name had my stepbrother off me in a heartbeat.

Dylan gripped my hand and yanked me into a sitting position as he straightened his button-down and smoothed his blond hair. He winked at me. The bastard.

When Dad didn't show up in the doorway, I knew it was the 'come here' sort of call.

"I have to go."

"Later," Dylan whispered.

Not if I can help it. Dylan had taken one youthful mistake committed years ago, and turned it into some sort of lifelong flame. No matter how many times I told him, he just didn't believe that twenty-five-year-old me wasn't the same as the foolish, needy nineteen-year-old I once was.

When my father and I had moved to Louisiana, we were despondent. Mom had left this world without saying goodbye or giving an explanation. Dad and I were adrift, trying to come up with some way to carry on even though our heart was gone, buried in the cold ground of a New York cemetery.

Dad eventually took a liking to Dylan's mother and tried to make a new start with her, and admittedly, her family fortune. Neither venture worked out and they divorced after only six months. Dylan and I were mismatched step-siblings if ever there were any. I painted and read. He loved sports and abhorred learning of any sort if it didn't have to do with X's and O's on a whiteboard.

Still, I was sad and desperately looking to feel something, anything, in the wake of my mother's death. Dylan was there and more than willing. So, I did something foolish. It was my first time—my only time—and I didn't exactly regret it afterward, I just didn't think about it. It was a non-event for me. That wasn't the case for Dylan, unfortunately.

I shook thoughts of him from my mind as I followed my father's voice to the back of the house and into his study.

Dad had sunk our last few dimes into this turn-of-the-century Victorian home. The whimsical façade was charming. The leaking ceilings and drafty windows? Not so much. Even so, it had been a safe place until Vinemont's tendrils had begun to invade, first with visits from investigators, then the arrest, then the searches. Vinemont had shown up each step of the way, reveling in the torment he inflicted.

For the millionth time that day, I hoped Vinemont would spontaneously combust. Then I strode into my dad's study.

The fire was crackling, and the room smelled of my

father's pipe. The atmosphere in that room always had a way of putting me at ease, making me feel safe. Even now, after all we'd been through, I still felt a familiar comfort when I walked in.

Along the back wall near the high windows, he'd arranged the draft paintings and sketches I hadn't sent to the local gallery. I'd caught him so many times just standing in front of whichever piece he'd decided to peruse for the moment, staring into it as if it held some sort of answer. My mother had taught me to paint. Maybe he was seeing her in the strokes and lines?

My feet hit the soft Persian rug that I used to play on as a child, bringing me back to the here and now. My father sat in his favorite wingback chair near the fire. The room felt fuller, somehow more occupied than usual, as if there was less air or not enough space.

Despite the crackling flames, the room was colder, darker. My familiar comfort drained away. Someone else was sitting in the matching chair facing my father, though I couldn't see who it was.

My pace slowed as I saw my father's stricken look. His wrinkled, yet still handsome face was pale, even in the flickering firelight. The first coils of dread snaked around my heart, constricting it slowly.

"Dad?"

Then I caught the scent of *him*. Whenever I passed him in the courthouse or when he came too close to where my father and I sat, I'd gotten a taste of this same scent. Woodsy and masculine with a hint of some sort of sophisticated tinge. My knees threatened to buckle but I kept going until I stood behind my father's chair and faced my enemy.

Vinemont's cold gaze appraised every inch of my body. "Stella."

I'd never heard him say my name. He spoke it with his signature arrogance, as if just uttering the word was somehow beneath him.

I scowled. "What is this? What are you doing here?"

"I was just discussing a business arrangement with your father. He doesn't seem inclined to accept my terms, so I thought I would run them past you. See if I got a different result."

"Get out," I hissed.

He smirked, though there was no joy in his eyes, just an inscrutable coldness that radiated out and made my skin tingle.

"I think you should leave." Dad's voice broke on the last word.

"Do you, now?" Vinemont never took his eyes from me. "Before I've had the chance to give Stella the particulars?"

I put my shaking hands on the back of my father's chair. "What are you talking about?"

"Nothing. Mr. Vinemont should be leaving." My father's voice grew a bit stronger.

"Y-you can't be here talking to my father without his attorney." I forced the tremor to leave my voice. "I know the law, Vinemont."

Vinemont shrugged, his impeccable dark gray suit rising and falling with the movement. "If you aren't interested in keeping your father out of prison, then I'll go."

He didn't move, simply watched me with the same dark intensity. Goosebumps rose along the back of my neck and shoulders.

What is this?

"What do you mean?" I asked. "How?"

"As I was just explaining to your father, I have a certain deal to offer. If you accept it, then he'll stay out of prison. If not, then he'll be going away for the maximum sentence—fifteen years."

"A plea deal? But you've refused this whole time to make any deal at all." My voice rose, anger influencing every word. "You were in the papers, telling anyone and everyone that you would do nothing short of seeing my father rotting in prison."

"Plea deal? I never said anything about a plea deal. I didn't realize you were this foolish." He steepled his fingers and canted his head to the side. He looked like Satan, the firelight dancing along his strong features. "No, Stella. I already have a conviction, nothing left but sentencing for him. And I have no doubt he'll get the max. I've made sure of it."

He spoke as if I was a small, slow child in need of extra after-school help.

"Then what? What are you offering?" My hands fisted, my fingernails digging into my palms. "And what do you want in return?"

"Ding ding ding, she finally catches on." His smirk grew into a wicked grin that chilled every chamber of my heart. His teeth were even and white. If there had been actual warmth in the smile, he would have been beautiful. Instead, he was the monster from my nightmares.

"The deal is simple. Even simple enough for you to understand, Stella." He reached into his inner suit coat pocket and drew out a folded sheaf of papers with some sort of wax seal. "All you have to do is sign this and your father will never see the inside of a prison cell."

"No. I've heard enough. Get out of my house." My father stood and came around the chair to stand by my side.

Vinemont finally tore his gaze from me and glowered at my father. "Are you certain, Mr. Rousseau? You do realize that a Louisiana prison is hell on earth as it is, but I have ways to make it even more unbearable. Cell mates and such? It would be a shame for you to get paired with a violent—or amorous—sort, especially at your age. You wouldn't last long. Maybe a month or two until you broke. And after you're broken, well, let's just say the prison system isn't exactly known for spending medical dollars on old, decrepit thieves."

"Get out!" My father's voice rang out stronger than I'd ever heard it, even as he trembled next to me.

Vinemont's smile never faltered. "Fine. See you in court."

He tucked the papers back into his coat, rose, and strode from the room. Confidence permeated his movements as he stalked out like some big, dangerous animal. The sureness of his words, the conviction of his gait left me feeling at once chilled yet burning to know why he'd come.

What the hell is going on?

When he was gone, I was finally able to take a full breath. I clutched the back of the chair. "What was that?"

My father pulled me into his chest, his familiar smell of tobacco and books cutting through Vinemont's more seductive scent. He was quaking violently. "No. Nothing. Forget about it. About him."

"What did he want? What was in those papers?"

"I don't know. I don't care. If it has anything to do with you, I don't want it. I don't want him near you."

I leaned away and looked into my father's eyes. He didn't meet my gaze, only watched the fire behind me the same way he would stare into my paintings. He studied something far away, past the flames and the bricks and the mortar.

Fatigue was written in every line on his face. Not even the flickering orange glow could hide how drained, how frightened he truly was. He hadn't looked this haunted since the night he found me lying on the floor, almost two years ago. I rubbed my eyes, trying to erase his fear and the memories from my mind.

He let out a labored groan and fell back against the chair.

"Dylan!" I called.

My stepbrother appeared in the doorway within moments. "What's going on? Was that the dick prosecutor I passed in the hall?"

"It doesn't matter, just please help Dad to his room. He needs to rest."

"No, no. I'm fine." Dad clutched me to him again, his grasp weaker, fading. "I love you, Stella. Don't forget that. No matter what happens tomorrow."

I forced my heart to stay together. If it shattered, I would be of no use. I couldn't become a quivering heap of regret, not yet. Not until I found out what Sinclair Vinemont wanted from me.

The Complete Trilogy Now Available

Counsellor, Magnate, & Sovereign

ROMANTIC SPORTS COMEDY
BY CELIA AARON & SLOANE HOWELL

Cleat Chaser

Kyrie Kent hates baseball. She hates players even more. When her best friend drags her to a Ravens game, she spends the innings reading a book... Until she gets a glimpse of the closer—a pitcher who draws her like a magnet. Fighting her attraction to Easton Holliday is easy. All she has to do is keep her distance, avoid the ballpark, and keep her head down. At least, all that would have worked, but Easton doesn't intend to let Kyrie walk so easily. When another player vies for Kyrie's attention, Easton will swing for the fences. But will Kyrie strike him out or let him steal home?

***

EROTICA TITLES BY CELIA AARON

Forced by the Kingpin
Forced Series, Book 1

I've been on the trail of the local mob kingpin for months. I know his haunts, habits, and vices. The only thing I didn't know was how obsessed he was with me. Now, caught in his trap, I'm about to find out how far he and his local cop-on-the-take will go to keep me silent.

Forced by the Professor
Forced Series, Book 2

I've been in Professor Stevens' class for a semester. He's brilliant, severe, and hot as hell. I haven't been particularly attentive, prepared, or timely, but he hasn't said anything to me about it. I figure he must not mind and intends to let me slide. At least I thought that was the case until he told me to stay after class today. Maybe he'll let me off with a warning?

Forced by the Hitmen
Forced Series, Book 3

I stayed out of my father's business. His dirty money never mattered to me, so long as my trust fund was full of it. But now I've been kidnapped by his enemies and stuffed in a bag. The rough men who took me have promised to hurt me if I make a sound or try to run. I know, deep down, they are going to hurt me no matter what I do. Now I'm cuffed to their bed. Will I ever see the light of day again?

Forced by the Stepbrother
Forced Series, Book 4

Dancing for strange men was the biggest turn on I'd ever known. Until I met him. He was able to control me, make me hot, make me need him, with nothing more than a look. But he was a fantasy. Just another client who worked me up and paid my bills. Until he found me, the real me. Now, he's backed me into a corner. His threats and promises, darkly whispered in tones of sex and violence, have bound me surer than the cruelest ropes. At first I was unsure, but now I know – him being my stepbrother is the least of my worries.

Forced by the Quarterback
Forced Series, Book 5

For three years, I'd lusted after Jericho, my brother's best friend and quarterback of our college football team. He's never paid me any attention, considering me nothing more than a little sister he never had. Now, I'm starting freshman year and I'm sharing a suite with my brother. Jericho is over all the time, but he'll never see me as anything other than the shy girl he met three years ago. But that's not who I am. Not really. To get over Jericho – and to finally get off – I've arranged a meeting with HardcoreDom. If I can't have Jericho, I'll give myself to a man who will master me, force me, and dominate me the way I desperately need.

***

A Stepbrother for Christmas
The Hard and Dirty Holidays

Annalise dreads seeing her stepbrother at her family's Christmas get-together. Niles had always been so nasty, tormenting her in high school after their parents had gotten married. British and snobby, Niles did everything he could to hurt Annalise when they were younger. Now, Annalise hasn't seen Niles in three years; he's been away at school in England and Annalise has started her pre-med program in Dallas. When they reconnect, dark memories threaten, sparks fly, and they give true meaning to the "hard and dirty holidays."

Bad Boy Valentine
The Hard and Dirty Holidays

Jess has always been shy. Keeping her head down and staying out of sight have served her well, especially when a sexy photographer moves in across the hall from her. Michael has a budding career, a dark past, and enough ink and piercings to make Jess' mouth water. She is well equipped to watched him through her peephole and stalk him on social media. But what happens when the bad boy next door comes knocking?

Bad Boy Valentine Wedding
The Hard and Dirty Holidays

Jess and Michael have been engaged for three years, waiting patiently for Jess to finish law school before taking the next step in their relationship. As the wedding date approaches, their dedication to each other only grows, but outside forces seek to tear them apart. The bad boy will have to fight to keep his bride and Jess will have to trust him with her whole heart to make their happy ending a reality.

F*ck of the Irish
The Hard and Dirty Holidays

Eamon is my crush, the one guy I can't stop thinking about. His Irish accent, toned body, and sparkling eyes captivated me the second I saw him. But since he slept with my roommate, who claims she still loves him, he's been off limits. Despite my prohibition on dating him, he has other other ideas. Resisting him is the key to keeping my roommate happy, but giving in may bring me more pleasure than I ever imagined.

***

Zeus
Taken by Olympus, Book 1

One minute I'm looking after an injured gelding, the next I'm tied to a luxurious bed. I never believed in fairy tales, never gave a second thought to myths. Now that I've been kidnapped by a man with golden eyes and a body that makes my mouth water, I'm not sure what I believe anymore. . . But I know what I want.

About the Author

Celia Aaron is the self-publishing pseudonym of a published romance and erotica author. She loves to write stories with hot heroes and heroines that are twisty and often dark. Thanks for reading.

CPSIA information can be obtained
at www.ICGtesting.com
Printed in the USA
LVHW080746261122
734074LV00054B/4601